Nima Shamloo Ahmadi, known as Young Author, born in 2006, is an Iranian poet, author and English translator, who studies humanity in Bournemouth, England. He began translating some English short stories and after compiling a book, turned to literary activities. Some of his works include:

1. ***The Gray Mind*** (A Collection of Short Stories)
2. ***Satanic Temptations*** (A Collection of Short Stories)
3. ***Paradise of Blame*** (A Collection of Short Stories)
4. ***Muddy Boots*** (Translation of 15 Great Short Stories from English to Persian)

Dedicated to my dear teacher, Majid Karimi as an international author, whose writing style inspired me.

Nima Shamloo Ahmadi

THE GRAY MIND

Dedicated to my dear teacher

Abi

I hope you enjoy reading my book

26 April 2023

AUSTIN MACAULEY PUBLISHERS™
LONDON · CAMBRIDGE · NEW YORK · SHARJAH

Copyright © Nima Shamloo Ahmadi 2022

The right Nima Shamloo Ahmadi to be identified as author of this work has been asserted by the author in accordance with sections 77 and 78 of the Copyright, Designs and Patents Act 1988.

All rights reserved. No part of this publication may be reproduced, stored in a retrieval system, or transmitted in any form or by any means, electronic, mechanical, photocopying, recording, or otherwise, without the prior permission of the publishers.

Any person who commits any unauthorised act in relation to this publication may be liable to criminal prosecution and civil claims for damages.

This is a work of fiction. Names, characters, businesses, places, events, locales, and incidents are either the products of the author's imagination or used in a fictitious manner. Any resemblance to actual persons, living or dead, or actual events is purely coincidental.

A CIP catalogue record for this title is available from the British Library.

ISBN 9781398466302 (Paperback)
ISBN 9781398466319 (ePub e-book)

www.austinmacauley.com

First Published 2022
Austin Macauley Publishers Ltd®
1 Canada Square
Canary Wharf
London
E14 5AA

I would like to express my special thanks of gratitude to my dear teacher, Majid Karimi, as an international author, whose writing style was developed in me. Also, to the book illustrator, Ms Armaghan Alimorovat.

Table of Contents

Preface	11
Cohen	13
Painter Artist	18
Roundtable	22
Strong Waves	29
Suit	36
Forbidden Room	42
Senior Official	48
Commander	54
Survivors	60
Rejected	65
Dream	71
Luxury Mansion	76
Endless Waiting	81
Futile Attempt	86
Castle of Panic	91
Years Later	99

Preface

The present book, called *The Gray Mind* (a collection of short stories), is taken from the daily conditions of every human being that he sometimes encounters during his life and is considered as a great challenge for him. But why humans find themselves in such a critical situation is a reflection of the behavioural complexities that lead them to a world far removed from individual imagination and to a world that is more like hell that endangers their peace of mind.

In this book, the author has made every effort to portray these conditions and to show that human beings are victims of conditions left to us by the superstitions and wrong frameworks of our predecessors. The author's attempt is simply to use the smallest spaces and the least characters to achieve the greatest concepts, which in today's terminology manifests itself as minimalism.

Finally, I would like to thank my dear teacher, Majid Karimi as an international author, whose writing style was developed in me.

I hope you enjoy reading this collection.

Nima Shamloo Ahmadi
December 2020

Cohen

Cohen

He put on the special clothes of the temple. After years of practice and austerity, he was able to achieve this high position. He was wearing a yellow dress and a beautiful necklace around his neck. Tall and with a kind of maturity on his face, he climbed the steps of the temple and entered. There was a big party and many guests were present. In fact, it was because of him that he was able to go through hard training and become a member of the Cohen. Flowers adorned the temple, and the fragrance of the flowers pervaded the temple. Along with the scent of the flowers, the scent of incense wafted into the corners of the temple. A big temple that was always being built and getting bigger. A temple that welcomed people who brought their requests there and hoped to reach them. In the middle of the temple hall, where the Cohens gathered, was a table with a variety of food, and in the other corner, people were playing religious music. Candles were lit in the corners of the temple, giving the hall a pleasant light. There were beautiful and ancient paintings on the walls of the temple. The temple stood on tall, massive pillars, and long curtains covered the windows. After the ceremony, the High Priest was to give a speech and then hang the sacred earring, which was made of pure gold, on Cohen's ear, and after drinking the Holy Grail, introduce him as the new Cohen of the city. A ceremony was held for Cohen in each city to introduce him to the people and to take better care of their affairs. A great ceremony was held in front of the Holy Orb and they sacrificed for this magnificent event by the order of the High Priest and to bless. However, someone who has been able to reach this position after years of training deserves more than this. The happy crowd gathered and clapped and shouted, rejoicing that such a person had become worthy of Cohen. They considered it auspicious because it could bring them a glimmer of hope. For this reason, and thanks to this event, gifts were brought to the Holy Orb, which was in a special place, and placed in front of it. Gifts, which included food, drink, and jewellery, were usually taken to the temple treasury after the ceremony and, by order of the High Priest to be used in times of need, and other food was distributed among them. A group of Cohens took turns guarding the Holy Orb with great care and did not take their eyes off it, and this adds to the importance of the Holy Orb. People in groups of seven came in special costumes to the Orb and then whispered their wishes under their lips and handed over their gifts to the guarding Cohens and then left and gave their turn to the next group and waited for their prayers to be answered. Sometimes a long, orderly line was created for this purpose. Especially when Cohen was being elected and the High Priest had come to the city. The Cohens were known among the people for their simple life, which is why they were more eager to bring gifts to the Holy Orb. Everyone brought a gift to the best of their ability.

For the High Priest, customs were the most important issue, and the ceremony continued even in the worst of times when there was sometimes famine and drought, and the people not only did not protest but demanded the performance with all their might. Even when poverty and helplessness made things doubly difficult for them or natural disasters happened, he could not postpone the ceremony. They were confident that the temple Cohens would save them with the help of a Holy Orb. For this reason, they patiently collected more gifts and came to the Cohens for help. The Cohens also promised them better conditions.

The ceremony began. Young Cohen, while glancing at the crowd, slowly climbed the stairs and came to the stand, standing next to the High Priest. He stared at the enthusiasm of the people. The people were full of excitement and shouted with joy. He felt responsible. He wanted to do something for them. He smiled with satisfaction at the crowd. It was as if he knew what he wanted.

He had thought of everything. At the same time, the High Priest took Cohen by the hand and raised him as his successor and representative in that city. Then it was Cohen's turn to speak. He was to deliver his first speech with firmness among the people. Soon everyone's eyes were on Cohen's mouth, waiting to hear something other than Cohen's promises. They just wanted to be saved. Silence was everywhere.

Cohen began his speech as follows, "We are looking for a world in which there is no more poverty and misery, violence and enmity, ignorance, war and bloodshed; a world without terror, and without hypocrisy. A world that no longer requires sacrifice. And human beings are free to live as they please, without harming each other.

The world that human beings have been looking for, for a long time. A world where no one is superior to another and everyone steps forward for a common goal. A world where no one owns another. A real-world free from hypocrisy. A world where the needy do not need customs to meet their needs. Now pick up your presents and return home. You need these gifts more than a Holy Orb."

Silence spread everywhere. In front of the others, he came down the stairs and sat down with a smile around the table that had been prepared for him. They brought him a drink to refresh his throat. He took it and put it to his mouth and drank a sip of it while watching the High Priest and the others. Then, in disbelief, he closed his eyes and fell on the table. At that moment, the High Priest stood and addressed the crowd, saying, "The punishment for anyone who disrespects the sacred sphere and its gifts, is death. He himself chose this path and the Holy Orb led him to the brink of death."

Painter Artist

Painter Artist

She looked at the dirty dishes in the sink. At the same time, she turned her head and looked at the laundry basket, which was full of glamorous clothes that she wore every night and went to night parties. She looked around. It was grey everywhere, her eyes falling on the mirror attached to the wall. She went to it. She looked at it. She saw herself in it. She stared deep into her eyes. Put her hands on her hair. She was more tired than she seemed, a bruise on one of her hands caught her eyes, and tears encircled up in her eyes. Really, why did she do this? But was it any different? She had chosen her path. The path to darkness and there was no turning back. To relieve her pain, she went to the clothes to forget her pain. This was not the first time she had such a feeling, but apparently this time it was different. She took her clothes from the basket and went to the laundry, but she could not concentrate. Something inside was bothering her.

Sometimes she thought maybe he was right. Maybe it was better to listen to her painter friend and pay attention to him. In this way, he was not bothered, nor did she have any doubts.

But this was the path she had chosen and there was no way back. Her painter friend had tried hard to dissuade her from what she was doing, but she thought to herself that she had no choice but to do so. She sat down on the chair as impatiently as possible. She never wished it was a night to wear those ridiculously luxurious clothes. The clothes she had hidden her true self under. Her thoughts were disturbed. She did not forget the moment of the last argument she had with her painter friend. She was sure that her painter friend really loved her and looked at her beyond a normal feeling. The ticking of the clock filled the room, and she listened to it for no apparent reason. Suddenly, she heard a knock on the door as if someone were knocking angrily. Unconsciously, she jumped up and went to the door. She stood behind the door. She did not have the courage to open the door. It was as if she had been waiting for news since the beginning of the day. She convinced herself and grabbed the door handle and opened the door. In front of her stood a tall man with a long beard and dishevelled hair, wearing a hat. She stared into his eyes. She was sure she had seen him somewhere before. Her guess was absolutely correct. She was the postman painted by her painter friend, and she remembered his painting on the walls of the painter's house. He was just like a painting, and that portrayed the ability of his painter friend. The two stood silently in front of each other, and neither dared to say a word. They both stared at each other silently and neither of them had the courage to say a word. Suddenly, the postman took a box out of his bag and held it out to her. The box was stained red with drops of blood stained on its cardboard walls. She looked at the postman's hands. They trembled. There were tears in his eyes. She noticed that the postman did not even want to look at her.

It is as if he knew what had happened and knew all the blame on the part of the woman. Anyway, he had spent a lot of time with her painter friend and known him very well. The woman could not wait any longer. Apparently, she wanted to end the meeting as soon as possible. She grabbed the box palely and at the same time, her hands became red. In fact, her hands smelled of blood. Pull the box inside. Immediately, without saying a word, she slammed the door shut on the postman and leaned against the door, moaning and seeing tears streaming down her face. Some time passed like that. Until she regained her energy and went to the table in the middle of the room and put the box on it and sat down on the chair, tired. She could guess what was inside the box. For a long time, her painter friend spoke of voices whispering in his ear that bothered him. In fact, there was probably no sound, and this was the news he heard from his love, and he could not bear to hear it. Now she saw her tears falling on the box and giving it life again in the colour of dried blood on the box. She put her hands to her face to wipe it. The dirt on her hands and face was now full, and the smell of blood emanating from her was everywhere. She picked up the box and carried it close to her. She knew his beautiful handwriting. She read, "A Gift from the painter, a piece of my body." She brought his lips to the box and kissed it. Then she put it in a box that held her valuables. She did not even want to open his gift.

Roundtable

Roundtable

The bell rang. The host hurried to the door, opened the door and showed the way to the guests. The guests also entered and soon stared at the space inside the house. The wooden houses that were old made it beautiful. The guests were sitting on the wooden furniture of the house and a brown wooden table was in front of them. It was full of engraved and mysterious engravings that everyone who looked at it, was thrilled and engaged every spectator and depicted the art of carpentry. One of the guests was staring at the table so that he might be able to find the mystery inside the table. A mystery that had strangely stunned him. Suddenly, the host placed a glass and pitcher of water with a tray of fruit on the table and caught his attention. The guest also thanked the host.

The guest began to say, "Don't you want to sell this wooden house and buy a new one like me? If I were you, I would sell this house and buy a modern, well-equipped house."

"Anyway, this is a nice, good house where I spent my childhood years. At the same time, we feel comfortable here," said the host.

"Do you have the same old car? I remember you wanted to buy a new car a few months ago," the guest said. "We went to the car dealership together. Whatever I insisted on, you did not buy it and said I did not have enough money to buy it. You were all satisfied. I bought the same unique car that I offered you for my wife. Last week, only one model remained. When I found out, I bought it in a hurry. My wife was very happy and said that no one has such a husband. I was proud of myself at that moment. If you bought a car at a time when it was cheap, your wife would be both very happy and it would have been very profitable. But now that time has passed and we cannot go back to the past. You have to think about the future, even today! Like me, you have to anticipate the future and plan for yourself. See how wisely I look at economic issues? I buy whatever my wife wants, I even bought a set of gold and two rings for my wife last week. In fact, life means this. It means knowing what to do. During this time, I bought everything I thought would make inflation worse. Now you can see who is successful. How I told you to come and buy a property? You did not listen. You say these are not good things. Everyone lives that way now."

The guest and host children went to the room and started playing. They were wrestling. The host was afraid that the children would hurt each other and cause trouble. He even warned the children several times, but the children did not listen.

"Please help yourself," said the host.

The guest nodded in agreement. He took the pitcher of water and poured a sip of water into his glass. He raised the glass and held it to his dry, cold lips. He drank the water and felt better. Then he picked an apple and peeled it. He wanted to say more about his life, sell, show off and cover up his inner weaknesses. In fact, he saw the host as a rival who could not compete with him. The host was a dignified and respectful man and had a special social status. His goal was to show the abilities that made him superior to the host. He had succeeded so far. Because he saw the frown on the host's face. So that the guest's wife, children and the host himself noticed this frown. Cold sweat settled on the host's face. He was afraid that these frowns might upset everyone. The host, who wanted to control the party, pointed to the painting above the roundtable.

"This beautiful painting came to me a few hundred years ago. This painting is so valuable that it cannot be priced," said the host.

The guest smiled and said, "That's why you are not rich. You spend all your wealth on books. See, your libraries are full of books. What good is it? You could buy a house and a car instead of books. You say it increases information: What is the use of increasing information, what does it matter who was on earth two hundred years ago and what was he doing? What do you want from books? What did you learn from all these books? What happened to all the philosophy you read? If you only checked the prices a little, you would be more successful now. I'm your friend, that's why I'm saying this. I'm heartbroken why my friend is so simple. Although I do not read books, I am more successful than you. The book is for those who do not even know what they want to do. Instead of books, I put decorative accessories in my shop window and I enjoy every time I look at them. Now it is true that you can only become a writer by reading a book, but who reads your books? Have you ever thought about these things? If you had worked like me and invested in something instead of reading books and writing, you would have become a millionaire like me."

The host wanted to answer him, but the guest continued, "With all these books, have you had a useful life for your wife and children? Have you thought about them? I have bought whatever I wanted for my children, but you only have two toy cars and several books. You have taken them for granted.

You want to make them miserable like you. I have taken my family on European trips. But do you have a passport? You have not been to even the weakest countries. I am trying to send my child abroad to study, but what about you? Do you not want your children to be happy? Do you want to keep buying books again? Another, the books are out of date. Who reads books since the system and conditions of the country have changed? Everyone is thinking about their profit. No one has mercy on anyone else. You should not have mercy on anyone. The time of mercy has passed. Compassion was for the past. You have to be careful not to become a victim to others. This holiday again, I want to take my family on a trip around Europe. If you have money, you can come with me."

The host's wife raised her eyebrows and showed her that she wished he had thought a little about them. Seeing that the situation was unfavourable, the host invited the guests to the dining room. Everyone pushed aside the roundtable chairs and sat down. The host, with the help of his wife, was preparing the food on the table. They set the table. Different dishes were on the table. Everyone who looked at the dishes wanted to start eating right away. The host introduced the dishes to the guest and asked him to start. The guest thanked the host. Suddenly, his eyes fell on a painting that actually looked like a puzzle and had a strange design. The guest stared at the painting for several minutes, wondering how some people lived with such strange and complex behaviours. The host noticed the strange looks of the guests on the painting. The host called the guest and said, "The food is getting cold. Eat some of it." The guest agreed with the host and began to eat. His mind was on the painting. He did not know what he was eating. He was completely confused and did not understand the host's behaviour. He went to the drinks, poured himself a glass and drank it. He got better, he never looked at the painting carefully, he was delighted with the art of the painter that he had painted.

The guest asked the host, "How many specimens of this painter can be found in the market?"

"This is the only work outside the museum," the host said. "This painting has been circulated among our family for several hundred years, and, after me, this painting reaches my child and then his child. I will never sell this expensive painting. These works of art can never be priced."

The guest laughed mockingly and said, "What does it matter to have this painting when you have no peace of mind for your life or money to meet your needs? I do not really understand your behaviour anymore. They are very strange."

They had finished all their food. The host, his wife and his child were gathering around the table when suddenly his eyes fell on the drawings of the roundtable. He was thrilled by the beauty and mystery of the house. He was going crazy. He could not say anything. The host, looking down at the guest, put a smile on his face. The host called the guest and said, "Don't you want to sit with us?" The guest quickly got up and walked over to them.

The guest began to speak. "Have you made your decision? Do you want to go abroad with us or not? I can help you a little financially. Just tell me. That's enough. That way your families will have a chance to see abroad and it will be an interesting experience for them. We will too. We are not alone. It is good for your son too. He can see the world. Look, I have done everything for my son. Be like me, give whatever your son wants from you."

At the same time, the children shouted and cried. The host and the guest turned their heads towards them and looked at the children. The children were pulling out a toy car, and each wanted to own it. The host got up to separate them. But when he got up, the host boy left the toy car. The host and the guest went to the children to find out the reason for their quarrel.

"He liked my toy car, Dad," said the host child. "I wanted to give it to him, too. But he jumped on me and pulled it. He did not give me a chance to give him the toy car."

The guest looked at his child a little sadly and said, "My son, I bought you all these toys. Why were you looking for old toys?"

"I want this car too," said the guest boy, who cried. Everywhere was silent. The host boy then picked up his only toy and handed it to him. The guest, his face blackened, lowered his head and fell silent.

Strong Waves

Strong Waves

Strong waves hit the ship. No one could have imagined that this great ship would fail in the storm. There was still room for hope. The ship was standing and resisting. The captain did everything he could, but still, the captain's experience and tricks did not work. Lightning flashed across the sky. The captain had to go his own way so as not to drown in the sea of destruction. An unfortunate catastrophe was ahead. The ship was moving at a speed of fifty knots. This was the fastest way possible to get away from the storm. The captain trembled with anxiety because he considered himself responsible for the lives of all the sailors. Finally, he ordered the sailors to lower the sails and prevent them from being broken. He looked at the senior officer to calm the sailors and ordered the watchman to search for the land or island across the sea. Everyone was working hard. But things did not go as expected. Suddenly, a large wave hit the ship and threw several people into the sea. The sailors picked up the lifeline and went to the ship's railings, staring at the raging water in search of them. They found two people waving in the roaring waves, shouting even though no one could hear them. They quickly hooped them up and pulled them up with difficulty. There were no other people who fell into the sea. The captain ordered the other men to take refuge on the deck so that the water would not carry them away. This was not the first time the captain had been in such a situation, but this time he was so frightened that he even forgot to shake his hand. Everyone was struggling to save themselves. Of course, with the damage done to the ship at every moment, the conditions for escaping from this predicament became more difficult. Suddenly, lightning struck the main mast of the ship, which was still standing. The observer, who was standing on top of it to assess the situation, fell down and fell into the sea in the shortest possible time. These images questioned the sailors' hopes at all times. Fear gripped them, but they had no choice but to save the ship. They had to keep the ship afloat. Ships that had to travel with great effort had to be rescued.

Suddenly, the roar of the ship shook everyone. A sailor shouted that the ship had been punctured. Many parts of the ship were destroyed. The captain shouted to try to control the situation. He asked for more help so that everyone could cover each other. Everyone had to work to save themselves and each other. The sailors did their best. They went to the hole of the ship and tried very hard to control it. The storm did not give them a moment to rest. The storm was getting worse every moment and the sailors were getting braver every moment. They hoped that the lifeboat, which they knew would not be affected by any storm, might arrive and save them from this situation. The great tribulation that only the giant lifeboats could get out of. The shipwreck sank in front of them and floated in the sea. They were very lucky that the storm had not yet wrecked the ship. The waves were bigger than usual. Disappointed, the captain picked up his weapon and knife. He dropped the bullets in his pocket. He gave each one a duty. He wanted to secretly get on the lifeboat and escape. He tore the rope holding the lifeboat with his knife and threw the boat down. Using a quick ladder, he went down and boarded the boat. Shortly afterwards, a severe thunderstorm struck the ship. The ship was sinking. The captain suffered a guilty conscience for not putting at least one person in the only lifeboat. He was sure that this would not have a happy ending for him. There were tears in his eyes. He was sorry. But he could not do anything else. Now he had to continue rowing and stay away from the ship, which was sinking at any moment. He must go to the land. He took the compass out of his pocket.

Using a compass, he could continue on his way and save his life. He had a plan with him. Of course, after all these years of sailing and experience, he could make his way to the land. But if he had used the map, he might have been able to get to a safer place faster and save his life.

Suddenly, he collided with a man who had fallen on a piece of wood and was holding himself hard. He was wearing a white dress. He must have been one of his sailors. The captain quickly paddled. He had to save at least one person to clear his conscience. Of course, he still did not know if he was alive or dead, but he had to go to his aid. It would be even better for him. The boat was approaching him at any moment. The captain reached him and dragged him into the boat with difficulty. His pulse caught carefully. He was still alive. He quickly took out the blanket in the lifeboat and threw it on him. He was happy with his action. He had to try to cheer himself up. Now that someone else was by his side, he felt happy. He caught the sailor's pulse again. It was as if he did not believe he was alive. He took a deep breath. Suddenly, the sailor woke up. The captain was happy. The sailor looked at the captain with a frown and surprise. "You must be hungry," said the captain. "Come and eat this canned meat in the lifeboat." The sailor began to eat. While eating, the sailor angrily asked why he had abandoned them and preferred to flee. The captain expressed regret and said,

"I also suffered a guilty conscience after this incident. But in reality, I could not do anything else. I saw you at sea. You wandered unconsciously on the sea. I saved you. You know very well that I could not have done it and let you die, but I did not. I came to your aid. You should not be angry and deem my work worthless. If I had not escaped, you would not be alive now. You should thank God that you are alive and sitting in front of me. Now we have to think about saving ourselves from this sea. From now on, we have to work in turns. I paddle for an hour, you do it for an hour. We do not have enough food and drinking water for a long time. I hope the lifeboat hears the news of our shipwreck and comes to our aid to search."

A few days later, they had no food. Both were dying. There was no hope. The captain and the sailor were praying. In fact, they could do nothing but pray. The captain shouted, "O God, if you hear my voice, send the lifeboat. I can no longer bear it. I know you have not forgotten us. I will close my eyes for ten minutes until the lifeboat arrives. Please send the lifeboat. Our only hope is to pray to you. If you send a lifeboat, I will dedicate my whole life to you. Just send a lifeboat." They both raised their hands. They begged for forgiveness. The sun was getting hotter by the minute. Suddenly, the captain thought. He remembered the day when everyone was warning him not to go to sea. The sea is very dangerous this season. But he carelessly thought of everything only for his purpose; a great goal that made him proud. But the captain was confident in his abilities. So he did so. His ability was beyond any season and sea. He was talked about everywhere in the streets and cities. In fact, it was the sailors who persuaded him to do anything. Scientists and meteorologists had told him that a major catastrophe would occur if he left. But he was willing to do so out of ambition. Everyone wondered how a man of this age and experience could not understand this danger when he knew that only luck could bring him out of this sea and out of such a storm alive. The last time only one person came out alive was a hundred years ago.

The captain boarded the ship, ignoring the professionalism of the people, and began to sail the ship. Everything was fine until the storm started. Suddenly, the captain felt someone splash water on his face. He opened his eyes and found himself in a small boat with a sailor. The sailor was able to catch a fish. He was very happy. The sailor tore the belly of the fish and cut a piece of fish and gave it to the captain. This fish was not enough for them. But at least they did not starve for hours. It was night. The sailor was paddling. The captain was praying. Suddenly, the storm began. The sailor and captain clung tightly to the boat. They had no hope; it was neither a lifeboat nor a ship. The captain was banging on the wall of the boat as to why he had done so. He wishes he listened to people. He had never been in such a situation before. The captain and the sailor were praying. They pursed their lips and continued in despair as tears welled up in their eyes. The heat and lack of drinking water had so drained their bodies that they both fainted. A few hours later, the lifeboat found them on the water and rescued them.

"I prayed and tried very hard. I was saved. I'm Wondered, whether my prayers were responded to or my efforts; or maybe your help and perhaps it was all just an accident," the captain said.

Suit

Suit

He got out of bed. He looked at his watch. He took a deep breath. He still had time. He had to go to the meeting. A meeting that determined his future. He made his bed and went to the bathroom. He took a shower. He had to be clean. He brushed his teeth a few minutes later. He had planned for everything so that he would not get into trouble. It took six minutes according to the plan.

He went to the papers for his speech. Read them again to practise. He realised that he was ready to speak at the meeting. He put them in a folder and put them in his bag. He went to the wardrobe. He wore a suit he had just bought. His hands trembled with stress. He could hardly breathe. He had to win. He went to the box of watches and chose one from his several beautiful watches, cheered himself up a bit, and went to the exit door. He decided to pick up the sheets and read from them until he got to the meeting. Left the house; he could not believe what he saw. He was holding his breath in surprise. The person he saw had strange clothes. A skirt like an umbrella and painted wood hung on it. It was like he was crazy. He continued on his way. He saw another person. He opened and closed his eyes. He could not believe he was wearing a tree leaf and a hat of a fruit basket. There were delicious fruits on it when he walked towards someone as if he wanted to serve someone. The man looked at him. He looked at his suit because everything had changed in one day; it was not possible. He wanted to get to the company quickly and end this horrible nightmare. He held his suit close together and covered his face as if he did not want anyone to see him. Everyone looked at him badly. It was as if he had sinned or ruined their rights. Everyone was wearing weird clothes. Even the policemen wore clothes like cookies and hats like cotton. The special police were wearing cake-like clothes with degrees of cotton and a hat of dark chocolate. In fact, he was the only one who wore a strange dress. Everyone was looking at him strangely. He did not know what to do. Either he had to go home and get rid of this nightmare, or he had to go to the company and not pay attention to others. He had a strange feeling. He had lost his confidence. Everyone was frowning at him. He could not do anything in those circumstances. He should not be disappointed. He should continue. He saw a peddler on the street corner wearing strange clothes and selling them. He decided to go to him and ask the price. He had some money with himself. He should see that he could buy those clothes with that amount of money. He asked the seller what the price was. The salesman, who was staring at him, replied, "Five walnuts." Suddenly, there was a deep shock.

"Five walnuts? This currency is not logical. I have other money with me. Can't I borrow those clothes and bring them back to you?"

"We only lend to those who have these clothes themselves, not to strangers who wear ugly clothes and make us uncomfortable with such clothes," said the peddler.

He was depressed. Why has everything changed today? What was wrong with her clothes? He always wore a suit. What happened today? Has the mood of the people changed or has the world changed overnight? Suddenly, a man in a knife-like dress came up to him and asked, "What are these strange clothes? What is their name? What is the name of the tailor? You have to say the name of the tailor to tell the police to punish him as soon as possible. I have never seen anything uglier and stranger than this dress. At least you were ashamed of your age. If you had bought our clothes instead, you would not be here now. See how people look at you?" It is as if the apocalypse has come, people have gone crazy. He repeated these words along the way. He saw a man whose beard was like a horn; red beard. It was as if he was watching the devil. He was dressed like a demon. A man stared at him with a cold, angry look. He had increased his walking speed. The closer everybody got to him, the faster he got and the more he covered with his hands. On the way, he saw a walnut. He picked it up and thought to himself that if he found a walnut again, he could buy clothes and become like the others. He put the walnuts in his pocket. He was getting closer and closer to the company. He was afraid that other people would dress differently and that the boss would get angry and fire him. He had never had so much panic and stress. He had a headache. He repeated to himself, *I like these clothes more. Why should I be influenced by people?* People only care about the work of others. In fact, they have no other job at all. Ignorance pervaded all people. Arrived at the company. He was worried that he might be fired. His whole life depended on winning today, but now he could be fired for a ridiculous outfit. This dress had signed his dismissal document. The air was getting warmer. He was going crazy. He talked to himself. He showed strange movements. He was staring at the entrance of the company; he could not stand it anymore. He had to take a risk. His brain was paralysed. He could not blink. He had to decide whether to go or not. It was a great danger. There was no way; if he left, he would be fired. If he did not go, he would still be fired. There were tears in his eyes. He decided to try his luck and see what was decided in his destiny. He entered the company. The staff started talking to each other until they saw him. What a strange dress he is wearing, he must have worn the right clothes. Everyone was frowning at him. He went to the boss's office. He saw the boss, the boss had a walnut skin dress that made him special. You could buy a city with the boss's clothes. He stared at the boss. His beard was braided into his hair. His brother wore a walnut dress. They were the richest people in the city. The boss asked about his clothes.

"Why did you wear this strange dress? I do not want to argue with you. You will not be hired and you are fired."

Suddenly he woke up.

He took a deep breath. He touched his body. He dried his sweat with a handkerchief next to it. He went to the bathroom and took a shower. He had a detailed plan. He picked up his toothbrush and rinsed his mouth for exactly six minutes. The program was very important to him. Nothing could disrupt his plan. He went to his closet. He opened the closet door. The strange clothes that were in his sleep and dream were now in the closet. He was surprised. His mind was disturbed. He searched everywhere. He did not find a suit. He had to wear these clothes. His dress was like a watch and his hat was like a cone. An earring hung from it. He went to the watch box. He saw a beautiful wooden watch with strange engravings. He dropped it. He went to his writings for the lecture. He practised a bit and put it in a lettuce folder, then put it in an orange peel bag. He put on his pointed, snake-like shoes and went out. He could not believe what he saw.

Everyone was wearing a suit.

Forbidden Room

Forbidden Room

He was walking down the street. A narrow, dark and cold street, with the corpses of dead rats and the stench that filled everywhere. A very scary place that scared every human being. He said to himself, "If I can travel in time, I can obtain and reveal many unattainable facts. After that, I can have an unattainable reputation." He carefully walked through the alleys to find his way to a dilapidated apartment where no one had been for years. In fact, no one was in that city. The disease had caused everyone to die. But several survived and migrated elsewhere. He remembered this place from his childhood. Every time he went there, he had to cover his whole body because of the disease so that it would not spread to him. It had been many years since the disease had penetrated that city and it did not leave. There was silence throughout the city, and only the sound of the wind accompanying his footsteps could be heard. Darkness did not frighten him. He continued on his way. He was determined to continue on his path. Suddenly, his eyes fell on the forbidden path. "This forbidden route will get me to my destination sooner," he said to himself.

He immediately remembered his father saying, "Never go that way. No one came back alive." In fact, his father was right. No one had returned from there. His curiosity increased every moment. Doubt took over his whole being.

He thought. "I have all the essentials of this dangerous journey with me. There is no need to worry anymore. I can go the forbidden way and find a new way," he told himself. Found himself entering a forbidden path; fear was in his heart. No one was there. Whatever was ahead was the corpses of humans that the mice were feeding on. Everything was destroyed. The trees were cut down and death and destruction were everywhere. His only happiness was that no one lived in that city anymore to harm nature. Nature of which nothing was left. He was happy about this, although he had no hope of returning to nature.

He continued to move. The further he went, the more frightening the path became. It is as if the monster of nature has risen and taken its revenge. Little by little, tall trees surrounded him. The heads that were nailed to the tree, and the blood that was spilt on the ground. He looked at the sky. The sky was gloomy. Although the moonlight shines on him. In fact, the only light he had was moonlight and he did not need any special lighting. He continued on his way. As it went, the moonlight shone through the trees. He remembered again when his father had urged him not to go there. He looked everywhere hesitantly. He was very scared; it was too late to return. The howls of wolves and predators made the place even scarier. The further he went, the darker the path became. Crows that crowed, and mice that passed under his feet. The large roots of the trees caused it to fall to the ground. His fear doubled. Suddenly, he saw a wooden hut in front of him. He stared at that hut. What was in that hut? He looked at the hut for a few minutes. He turned his head. He saw a wolf coming towards him quickly. He ran to the hut as fast as he could. He had no choice. The wolf was reaching for him. It was as if nature wanted to destroy him like everyone else. He thought to himself that nature does not give humans a chance and kills them all. Arrived at the hut. The door was closed. But with a strong stroke to the shoulder, it suddenly opened. He was amazed at how lucky he was to open the hut with the first strike. The wolf was almost one-step away from him. He took a deep breath and wanted to spend the night there; an old, two-story, dark cottage. In fact, he had no choice. Night had arrived. He felt cold. His eyes fell on the fireplace. The fireplace was almost close to the kitchen. He opened his bag. Hoping he brought a match with him. He was so upset that he could not find a match in his bag. He turned his bag again. Again, he found nothing. He went to the kitchen. He searched the kitchen cabinets. He did not find anything. There was only one cabinet left to explore. He opened it. He saw a match. He picked it up and went to the fireplace. It was a cold night. He opened the matchbox. There were only two matches left. He only had two matches. He picked up the sticks that had been placed by the fireplace. He went to the fireplace. He piled the sticks on top of each other and poured the oil next to the fireplace on the sticks. He took the match out of the box and tried his luck. The match did not light up. Fear set in his heart. There was only one match left. If this match did not light up, he would definitely die of a cold. Tried his last chance. The match was lit. He took a deep breath, but the wind blew the match out. Fear set in his heart. He knew he was dying of a cold. He decided to go to his bag and look at it again. He picked up his bag and went to the dining table. He spilt all his belongings on the table. He looked around carefully. Surprisingly, he found the match in his bag. He was happy and went to the fireplace. He lit a match and headed for the oil on the sticks. The fireplace was lit. He proudly admired himself. He thought about the fear he had a few minutes ago and laughed at it. He went to the dining table and picked up the can he had left and put it on the fireplace. He was hungry. He lit the candles of the hut. The can was ready. He went to the fireplace and picked it up with a piece of cloth. He took a spoon out of his bag and began to eat canned food. He ate so eagerly that if anyone was there, they would think he was eating canned meat. He had run out of food. He thought about how lucky he was and that he was still alive, despite the fact that his father had repeatedly warned him not to go the forbidden way. He wanted to sleep. He went to one of the rooms on the first floor. His eyes fell on the door of the room where the entrance sign was forbidden. Nothing mattered to him anymore. He boldly opened the whole room. He was holding his breath until the door opened completely. There was nothing but a bed and a table. He took a deep breath. Suddenly he saw a door on the floor of the room with a no-entry sign on it. He became anxious. He said to himself, "This door must be like all the doors I have opened." Each one had no entry signs, but nothing special happened. He also opened the door with curiosity. The ladder was there. He went down the ladder. It was as if the basement of the house had access to it from the first floor of the house. When he reached the bottom, he stopped breathing. He saw many corpses and inscriptions engraved on the wall. Strange writings that no one could read. He suddenly thought that maybe he would get stuck there and become like them. He was worried.

Meanwhile, someone grabbed him from behind and stabbed him in the back. "This is the punishment for anyone who comes to a forbidden room," he said in his ear.

Suddenly, he opened his eyes. He realised it was an illusion. He looked carefully at his body. No knife marks were seen. He began to flee in fear. He hurried up the stairs to the front of the hut. He runs to the newly established village. The branches hit him hard on the face. His face was bruised. His feet sometimes got stuck in the roots of trees. He was in a bad mood. He thought he would never reach the village. As if his father's words about the forbidden path were true. He increased his running speed. He thought someone was chasing him. He did not want to return to the restricted area. He understood that it was a great punishment to go crazy, because of knowing too much. He had no breath left. He fainted there. He regained consciousness and found himself in the hut again. He looked at his body, he was bleeding from his back. He did not run away, he lay there and waited for death.

Senior Official

Senior Official

The voices of the high-ranking officials were everywhere. Before the news broke, the trumpeters played the trumpet and the drums. People rush to the door or window to listen to the news. Whenever the drum sounded, there was good news. They had not received any sad news for years. This was usually news about celebrations. Eventually, the heralds stopped playing and started reading the letter.

"Attention, attention, by order of the senior official, everyone should attend the upcoming celebration that will take place tomorrow night. You can see that they care about the people. The senior official said that if someone does not attend the special celebration tomorrow night, he will be cursed. This celebration has been in our culture for many years and there is nothing and no excuse in front of it."

"There is no curse," said the young man suddenly with a laugh.

Silence was everywhere. Everyone frowned at him. "We warned about the curse. The choice is yours. But keep in mind that a fateful end awaits someone who does not attend tomorrow's celebration and ridicules it," the herald said.

The young man was always opposed to such celebrations. He insisted that there was no curse. By not attending the celebration, he wanted to prove that there was no curse and that all of this was the product of illusions and fantasies. Imaginations that have occupied people for many years. Several people agreed with him. He was happy to be able to inform at least a few people. He did not know what fate awaited him. All the people were afraid because the young man, by mocking these special celebrations, caused all the people to suffer an eternal curse. The people decided to gather the elders of the city to advise the young man. They did not want their many years of happiness to be destroyed and them to be in poverty again. The elders went with the people of the city to the young man's house. They knocked on the door. The young man opened the door and stared at the crowd in surprise. The elders greeted him, and the young man invited the elders of the city to his house as a tradition. There was still a look of surprise on his face. The young man took them to the reception hall of the house. The elders began to speak, "Young man. We have come here only for advice. You have a beautiful house, it refreshes us."

The young man thanked him. "People are tired of making fun of celebrations. You know, at one time a senior official cursed the city, and we are in poverty. Do you still not believe in the power of a senior official? Even the authorities get his permission to do things. You are the only one who makes fun of him. We know you do not believe in curses, but come to the party and do not anger the senior official. You have to be careful not to curse yourself or people."

"These are all born of fantasies." The young man said, "Even I, as a young man, know that all this is the plan of a senior official, you are afraid to say these things because you are afraid that the monthly allowance will be cut and the senior official will ruin you all. I just want to guide you and do not let ignorance cause you to fall behind. I never want to curse people forever."

The elders of the city stared at each other. Surprise ripples through them all. "When you were not born, we saw all these curses. They cannot be denied. Not even the rules of celebration can be denied. They were not written by an earthly creature," said one elder. "If you can, say something like these are rules."

The young man thought and could not say anything. "Anyone can write such rules. Just have a strong dictionary in mind."

The white beards of the city, not knowing what to say, frowned and left him. People asked the elders what the result was. Was he coming to the party?

"No," said the white-bearded man, "he is very stubborn. He never listens to what others say and only speaks for himself. He destroys us all." Other people were tired. He even rejected the letter that people had written to him. Eventually, the people decided to attack his house and destroy it. At night, people raided his house and smashed his valuables. The young man was terrified. He had never been so scared. People thought that maybe this was his curse for them to attack his house. So they decided to do it again. The next day came. A day of celebration, a day that everyone had been waiting for. Everyone was divided into different groups and waited for the senior official to come to them and guide them. All the people had gathered and only the young man was left to come. All the people were afraid that the young man might not come. Suddenly, the senior officer came and said, "I hope you are all here. As you know, not attending this celebration will curse you."

People did not hear anything out of fear. The guide ordered the people to move. There was still hope. Maybe the young man could reach them? After a while, they arrived at the hall. The young man had not come. They lost hope and went to the table to eat drinks and a variety of foods. Everything was fine. People forgot about the young man and were talking. The sound of whispers was everywhere when suddenly the senior official entered with the sound of a trumpet. Silence spread everywhere. The high-ranking official entered in a strange dress and shook everyone with his firm steps. "I hope you all are here," the senior official said. "Is there a young man whose absence has filled the whole city?"

The people replied with a little fear, "No, sir, he has not come."

The senior official slapped his hand on the table and said, "Did I not say that whoever did not come will be cursed? Have they underestimated my power?"

People said quickly, "No."

The senior official controlled his anger and then began his long speech. "As you know, this celebration is very important and all our blessings are from this celebration. No one should make fun of this celebration. If anyone does that, he will be cursed…"

The senior official let the people talk to each other. Everyone stared at the high wall of the hall with the flag of the senior official attached to it. There were countless officers guarding the high position and the hall. Everyone was eating or drinking. The senior official rose from his seat and walked out, which meant the celebration was coming to an end. They packed up and went home. The next day, people went to the young man's house to warn him of the senior official's anger at not taking traditional ceremonies seriously. But the door was open. They entered the house. They went everywhere well. The house was more ruined than before. There were bullet holes on the walls. They went to the second floor. Suddenly, they came across the dead body of a young man. Silence fell on everyone and everyone stared at him. "It was a punishment for not celebrating and disrespecting the old rituals. Get out of the house quickly so that you do not get cursed." Then they wrote on the door, *Cursed*.

Commander

Commander

"O people, from now on you are free, you are human, you must always be free. Freedom is a gift that God has given us. But the profiteers and the oppressors have taken this God-given gift from us and you; dear ones. Is there any other way but to fight these oppressors? All human beings must realise their worth and no one should depend on anyone else. The era of bullying masters is over. You feel free here. But is that enough? Isn't it better to think of a bigger mission? Look at the lands around us. How the tyranny of the wicked has enslaved innocent people? Will you support me in this way to save others from the bondage of the masters?"

Everyone was staring at the commander's mouth. In their hearts, they admired the commander as a freedom-loving and kind man. People praised him for his courage. In fact, he was the first commander to oppose the lords and set free the slaves. Although he was under pressure from them because he jeopardised their interests. Suddenly someone shouted from the crowd.

"Commander, we support you." Saying this sentence, people suddenly clapped for him and they repeated the same sentence with one voice. Meanwhile, the commander ordered his troops to prepare for battle and free the slaves and saviours of other lands. His army consisted of thousands of archers, several hundred cavalrymen, and several thousand men, and there were many people who volunteered for the job. At the command of the commander, all the armies were armed and some were responsible for carrying the catapults. There was a bloody war ahead of them. The commander had brave soldiers who were always ready for war and countless volunteers who could not bear to see other human beings enslaved. Nothing could stop this war anymore.

The slogan of the troops was freedom. After the commander visited his prepared troops, an order was issued to move, and since he was an intelligent man, he had previously sent a spy to that land to convey the military news and information of that country to the commander. After a few days of marching, they reached the land and found themselves in front of a high and strong wall, as if no one had been able to cross it. The spy, who was waiting for the commander nearby, reached out to him to give a history of the soldiers. He went to the commander's tent. The guards surrounded it. Asked for permission to enter. The commander greeted him and called him into the tent. Without any delay, the commander asked about the situation. The spy replied, "There was a difficult way to cross these walls. Archers are waiting for their victims on top of these walls. My suggestion is to use a catapult with fire, and then you can enter it from the side hills, which have been reduced in height and which the enemy does not control. But, Commander, there is a more important issue than this. Those who make up the enemy army are the slaves who do not know the truth of freedom and will fight against you. They do not even know who they are fighting for. Now you are still determined to help them."

The commander was silent for a few minutes, and perhaps the most painful part of the battle was that they did not know what they were fighting for. He answered to the spy, "They do not know what they are doing. They have not tasted freedom. That is why they do not have a proper understanding of liberation. We must be patient. You had better rest a little too. You must be very tired. I am proud of you. You have risked your life so much."

The commander came out of the tent. He prepared his troops and shouted, "O brave soldiers, free people, we are fighting for freedom! We will liberate all the lands. Wherever there are prisoners, we will rush to their aid. Now prepare the catapults. Prepare yourself for a tough battle. Hurry, the real victory is yours. By doing so, you teach your fellow human beings a lesson of sacrifice and freedom." The catapults were carried to the wall near the hill, and in a short time, the sky of the land was filled with fireballs that landed on the ground and set fire everywhere. A fierce battle broke out and the soldiers attacked the walls and at the same time, a rain of bullets fell on them. At the command of the commander, they raised the shields above their heads and reached the wall. The catapults were still destroying the wall. After a few hours, a group finally reached the top of the wall and stopped the enemy archers. Now the war had entered a new phase. They faced each other and there was nothing far from victory. The screams of the soldiers, one after another, stained with blood, filled the air. The people who had been laughing and eating until an hour ago were now lying motionless on the ground. The victory was near. The opening of the gate also guaranteed victory. The city had fallen and now the commander was the winner of this war. The news of the tyrant ruler being killed by his soldiers soon reached him, and this meant complete victory. One by one, the enemy soldiers laid down their weapons and surrendered. He brought his commander to his position and from there addressed all his companions, saying, "O people, I do not know why you supported someone who considers you a slave. I wish you knew that we came to save you. It is not too late. I know that you are free and that our intention in this war was to help you."

Suddenly, a voice rose in the crowd. He was one of those slaves who fought for his master with someone who wanted to save him. He came a little further and shouted loudly, "We are free, but who can give us bread and water? You have killed our masters, and now we feel helpless. We do not know what to do. We are used to this life and none of us complained. In fact, what difference does it make who we work for and call him master and meet our needs, or who are free to seek work and experience another kind of captivity? Yes, we have been set free. But now we have to take on another kind of slavery in front of you as the new commander of this land. If this means freedom, we would be satisfied with the same servitude, and now, on behalf of all the slaves who were captives of their masters, I declare that we welcome the great commander as the new master."

The commander listened in surprise to the representative of the slaves and had nothing to say in disbelief. His ears could not believe what he had heard, and he looked at each one of them, and after a moment's hesitation shouted,

"People! Do you all think so? Are you all accustomed to the cruelty of your masters? Many men have lost their lives in this way, and instead of appreciating, you called me a new master?"

The representative of the slaves, as if he had become bolder, smiled bitterly and mockingly turned to the commander's soldiers, saying, "Is it not that you have achieved freedom in your land? But you too, have come to the battlefield as slaves for your commander. Many of you have lost loved ones in this war. What difference does it make if we are slaves to our masters or supporters of a great commander who may be fighting for his endless fame? It is not better to go to our homes instead of freedom and such slogans and get used to a world away from war and strife. Your command may have been good for us, but again, we see nothing but servitude to a greater master. I wish there came a time when we humans experienced a life where no one called hero or commander wanted to save anyone. Now we will all be servants of your commander."

The commander had completely lost his credibility and did not want to be challenged anymore. Suddenly, he stood up and shouted loudly, "Arrest him! He does not know what he is saying. It is better for him to continue in the same slavery and servitude. The punishment for one who does not know the true meaning of help and freedom is captivity." Then he got up and left the town square.

Survivors

Survivors

The troops were on standby. There was a great war between humans and extra-terrestrials that the history of such a massacre had never seen. A decisive battle for land. Extra-terrestrials came into being with long, slender heads and bodies that no creature resembled. But he could read the fear on their faces. They were afraid of humans, even though they considered themselves superior to them. They were encamped near the armies of men. They were afraid to fight humans because humans could do whatever they wanted. They could also build a tool to destroy them. The man was seen as intelligent, having been able to inhabit the earth for thousands of years and drive them off the earth. Humans monitored their behaviour with advanced weapons and binoculars. Both had attained supernatural and magical powers. This could not be a normal battle. The history of the earth did not remember such a battle. Among humans, there were some who feared extra-terrestrials. Some humans left the camp out of fear and joined the extra-terrestrials. Some extra-terrestrials also joined humans out of fear. No one knew who would win this battle. It could have been a long battle. For this reason, they had prepared food for several years. The extra-terrestrials wanted to take back the land they had been taken from, to destroy humans, and to live on earth themselves. They had been planning for years. They even sent people to earth in the form of humans to control humans and study them. But man was determined and did not intend to leave the earth. He did not want to give way to extra-terrestrials so easily. That's why they had a lot of preparation. They had the most advanced weapons and powerful wizards. But they were unaware that the extra-terrestrials had also developed their supernatural forces and were ready for battle.

It was time for war, a strange and different war than ever. A war in which a lot of blood was waiting to be shed. The extra-terrestrials took off their wings and approached the humans. No one knew what their plan was. Humans, too, with the magical power they had acquired, grounded the extra-terrestrials with the words they uttered and the arrows coming out of the most advanced weapons. The extra-terrestrials could produce a terrible fire by waving their hands and setting fire to the human army. Humans also attacked them with bombs and gunpowder. Weapons that extra-terrestrials did not understand and did not know how to confront and defend themselves.

Humans, in the first stage of the battle, killed many extra-terrestrials and were happy. They did not believe that they had succeeded so far. The extra-terrestrials retreated a little and moved towards the river, and with a strange force, they opened the river and went to the other side of the river. Humans were all staring at this scene. A scene that instilled fear in the hearts of all human beings. The commander of the humans ordered the wizards to learn the trick and go to the river and open the river and not give extra-terrestrials a chance to rejuvenate. The commander was victorious in this field, no matter how he looked at it. Thousands of wizards stood behind the river and were able to open the river by sending magic. The great wizards also blew it up by sending strong energies. But they did not know that the extra-terrestrials went underground so as not to be harmed. The wizards moved to the extra-terrestrials. Open the magic book so that if a creature attacks them, they can take the book to him and be saved. They arrived at their camp. No one was there. The wizards felt that powerful energies were coming to this place. Suddenly, it exploded everywhere. The wizards recited a word, and with this word, some of them were able to survive in the fire. But many of them were killed and the bodies of many wizards were dumped on the ground. The wizards, who were happy until a few hours ago, were now dead. Several thousand wizards managed to escape, but hundreds also died. The wizards met with the commander of the army and the wizards' leaders and explained their defeat to the commander. The commander got angry and hit the table hard. He went outside the tent and looked at the river that was clear a few days ago. It no longer had the usual beauty. The corpses were immersed in it. He was confused and did not want to harm nature. But for the sake of the human future, the war had to continue. So he ordered his soldiers with strength and fortitude, and he himself put on armour and went to the field.

There were fires everywhere. The corpses were burning and the stench was everywhere. Winter was approaching. Humans did not have enough clothes for winter. The extra-terrestrials were also tired of war because they had suffered so many casualties. Humans tested extra-terrestrial corpses to perhaps find a weakness and defeat them. But they did not learn anything. It was as if they had no weaknesses. Research had even shown that they had the ability to recover damaged organs. The commander was worried and frustrated. He did not know what to do. So he intended to kill himself. But the wizards promised to help him. The day of battle was near. It was winter now. A winter in which even extra-terrestrials could not survive the oppressive cold. Few humans and extra-terrestrials remained. Some died from the cold, some from fear, and others from the war.

The war took on a new life. Both divisions began to send energy and each fought with all its might. A terrible war had begun. This was their last war. Nobody knew who would win the match. The heat of winter engulfed humans and extra-terrestrials, weakening their morale and power. The war was over. A limited number remained. The cold weakened their power and killed them. Extra-terrestrials and humans died from the cold, and their next generation returned to the life cycle. So no other creature was created, and other creatures continued to live in eternal peace.

Rejected

Rejected

He was called rejected. He was the son of an expelled court official who had an affair with an immigrant woman. He was called rejected because he lived in a land with special laws that did not allow authorities to have intercourse with immigrant women or to marry and have children with those who were not of their blood or descent. But some officials broke their covenant and did so secretly. If this became public, the officials who did so would be sent with their wives and children to a place reserved for the excluded, in other words, deported. Some people came every day to make fun of the rejected and looked down on them as a lesson to others. In fact, there were large, dry, tropical valleys with ruined houses from which no one survived and there was no hope of returning. People considered them human beings with demonic blood whose blood has lost its originality. There was little water or food to survive, and the authorities sometimes sent them out of pity. It was more like a hell that swallows the rejected. They were always in torment. There was no way to escape. There was a lot of care. Originally, there was a prisoner who had no way out. Some of them tried to revolt, but they could not, because there were guards there to prevent the revolt. In order to heal the pain of loneliness and rejection, they decided to build a temple with the little skills and equipment they had and to worship the holy sceptre left as a relic of their past. They wanted to build the building at first, out of sight of the guards, and this allowed them to unite. But they soon realised that the guards did not care what the deportees were doing, because most of them thought it was a hobby, and their job was simply to counter the deportees' revolt.

It took a long time until the temple was finally built. The number of people attending the temple was increasing every day. So they decided to determine their own destiny. It was time to fight the superstitions. They revolted, but this time with more unity. The guards tried to suppress the ousted rebels, but the clashes were more than they had imagined. The streets were covered in blood. The commander of the expelled was worried because he did not want many people to be killed. The corpses, which until a few hours ago had blood flowing in their veins, were now bloodless. The commander of the expelled could not sacrifice his main goal for the sake of a few people. A goal that he had been pursuing for many years. He stayed there for many years to witness such a day. A lofty goal that was considered a kind of realisation of the right. They were rejected because of their trivialities, and their only guilt was that they were either immigrants or considered officials who had relations with immigrants. He wanted to send a message to the people of his land that no one was superior to another and that the blood of all human beings was the same colour. They were not far from victory. The commander gathered the rejected and began his speech before the final attack. He took the sceptre and said, "Today is the last day of the battle. Let us unite and face them with one voice and gain freedom. With the help of this sceptre, we will win, and we will defeat the enemy." They attacked the guards. The commander of the rejected held the sceptre of their past as a sign of freedom and beat it to the ground, and this was the beginning of the final war. A miracle took place. With twice as much strength and motivation as ever, they fought for freedom and opened the way to the camp of the enemy army. The victory was theirs. The rejected shouted for joy, beheaded the corpses, and sent them to the ruler of the city where he had exiled them. But it was as if this was just the beginning.

Some time has passed. They had conquered the land from which they had been expelled, and now, thanks to the gift the temple had for them, they decided to renovate the temple structure and build a special place for the staff. They still had problems. The commander of the rejected worshipped in the sanctuary of the temple. There were fragrant incense sticks around the temple sanctuary that calmed the commander and helped him think better. After several hours of thinking, he finally made his decision. He quickly left the temple and ordered everyone to gather in the town square and bring him a sceptre. They brought a sceptre. He went to the town square and stood among the rejected. He beat the sceptre on the ground as usual. The commander said with a triumphant smile, "From now on, together as before, with unity, we can withstand all difficulties. We are no longer rejected and have become a liberated land; a rich and powerful land that we have reached with great effort. But people in other countries still call us rejected and our names are included in the map of lands. This is what makes us angry and annoyed."

To get rid of this issue, people brought food and gold for the holy sceptre every day to help them again. By order of the commander, all the gold was sent to the treasury to be used in case of emergency. The temple was getting bigger day by day and the number of its followers was increasing.

By the order of the commander, a memorial was erected for the slain monk so that the people would never forget him. He also asked for the holy sceptre to help create conditions that other lands would call civilised and no longer call them rejected. But this time he felt that the temple did not meet this need.

The night has come. The commander was asleep when suddenly his feet moved and he was walking towards the desert. He was scared. He could not command his feet to stand. Suddenly, he found himself holding a sceptre on the threshold of a cave; a large cave where there were many places to hide. He soon realised that he went there every night barefoot, unconsciously wandering the corridors as if to hide something. The other people were tired of him and did not want to lose their commander. The doctor was taken to him. "Tie him with a rope so he can no longer go anywhere at night. He is delusional. You have to think of other commanders." the doctor said.

But to no avail. The rope did nothing and he went to the cave. It was as if a supernatural force was pulling him into a cave, or maybe it was the sceptre that was taking him there. He was still looking for something in the corridors of the cave. Suddenly, his eyes fell on a strange book. He picked it up and read it. But he did not notice anything. He decided to take it to the moon. It took the moon. Suddenly, everything became legible. He lost control of his feet again and moved to his residence. He went to bed and suddenly fell asleep. When he woke up, he saw a book on the table. He could read it. He decided to talk to people about this book. He gathered the people together. Suddenly, he saw that everyone was listening to him with all their being. He thought to himself that maybe it was the effect of the book or maybe it was because of the sceptre he was holding. He introduced the book to the people. Everyone became more allied with him because of the book he wrote. The commander did not even know that he had written the book himself. He decided to go to the lands that they call rejected. He sent messengers. He saw how easily the king received him there. It was more like magic. It seemed beyond his mind. He was not content with this, and greed and excitement pervaded his whole being. He wanted to establish his empire all over the world. He moved to other lands, and with the magic he possessed, he subdued them as well, removing the names of the rejected from the map, and engraved his empire in the minds of the people. But old age did not give him a respite.

Dream

Dream

She entered the scene while tapping her foot on the ground. Many spectators came to the theatre to see the play. Excitement filled her whole being. The spectators were staring at the movement of her arms and legs. She unconsciously played her role and had no control over her movements. The hall lights were off and the projectors were shining directly on her face. It was as if she had just been sitting in a rocking chair behind the scenes, talking with herself. She remembered the words she had said to herself before the show. "I can't do the show right," she repeated to herself. She thought about the past for a few minutes. She laughed at why she had said such things in the past. She stopped her laughter so that the show would not be ruined. That was the only chance she had, so she did not want to lose.

There was a table with a pitcher of water and a glass next to the hall. After a short performance, she could go to the table and drink some water. She went to the table, drank some water and resumed the show. Her eyes fell on the rocking chair she was sitting on. Suddenly another light came on and this made it impossible for her eyes to see well. She put her hand in front of her eyes.

If she kept her hand over her eyes a little more, the show would be ruined. Suddenly, she concentrated and quickly continued to show, this was her only chance. The director was satisfied with her performance. The director watched everything and monitored the movements of the audience. She wondered what would happen if the director did not like her performance? Will she be fired and lose her life hope or will she stay and get more education? It had been a long time since the show. She was thirsty again. The show continued and she walked slowly towards the table. The show stopped for a few seconds. The spectators clapped for her. Her whole face was sweaty. She continued to show. She moved her hands like the wind in the sky. Everyone stared at this move and suddenly, everyone clapped for her involuntarily. Her excitement diminished. It seems that she has the experience of playing thousands of plays. No one had ever played the show well. She saw herself on the verge of becoming famous. She was dressed in white cloth and with comfortable shoes that could easily walk on stage. All these clothes were designed for her by the designer. She had no experience in acting, but she had a lot of talent for acting. She was very happy, because the show had only one actor, and that was her. She never thought of performing in such a crowd. A smile was still visible on the director's lips. She had little experience performing the play. She used to play in street theatre, but not many people came to see her play. But the director had found her in the street theatre.

She spun. Her eyes fell on the director. The director nodded and showed that he was very satisfied with the show.

He thought she would become the most famous actor in the world and could play alongside the best actors. Thoughts did not leave her head. In fact, she was just thinking, and the rest of the work was done by her hands and feet. She came to herself. She did not know where the show was. She did a few repetitive moves to remember the next moves. She fascinated everyone with her foot dance. Of course, she felt blackness in the audience. Some came just because of her, and some because of her art. Some came just to waste their time. With her movements and white clothes, she became like an angel who came to earth and performed a play. Everyone clapped for her. They cheered and wanted to take pictures with her. But taking pictures with her was a difficult task, the actors behind the scenes were jealous of her because the director paid so much attention to her.

The show was about to begin. A beautiful show that puts everyone's finger in their mouths. Sometimes the director and other actors behind the scenes also clapped for her. But she could not control the shadows sitting on the chair. The shadows wanted to hug him. Sometimes she mocked war and violence with her performance. Little by little, the lights came on. The theatre was in progress. She made her last move. Everyone clapped for her. Suddenly, she unconsciously bowed to them and left the scene. She went to the photography scene so that her fans could take pictures of her. Fans took pictures with her one by one. Sometimes shadows also took pictures with her. She hated shadows, but because they were also her fans, she had to take pictures with them. She posed for pictures with almost hundreds of her fans. She then went to her rocking chair behind the scenes. She closed her eyes and thought about everything that had happened. A few minutes passed. She opened her eyes. Suddenly, she found herself in the house where she lived. She looked around. Nowhere was it like a theatre stage. She realised that everything was just a dream and she had not played in any theatre. She decided to perform what she had dreamed of in her house without any spectators.

Luxury Mansion

Luxury Mansion

Twelve people were sitting around the table in the dining hall. The lady of the mansion was on one side and the gentleman on the other. A long table made of walnut wood and its beautiful engravings can be seen. On the table were two silver cups that barely illuminated the dark and eerie atmosphere of the dining hall. There were silverware and crystal glasses on the table waiting for the guests. Beautiful and expensive paintings were installed on the corners and walls of the dining hall, which gave a special view to it. On one part of the wall was a genealogy depicting the family origin of the lady of the house and a display of her authority. In another corner of the wall was a picture of a lady of the mansion with a special skill depicting her power, but there was no sign of the gentleman. The guests entered one by one, and the most important of them was the architecture that built this mansion in such a mysterious way that after a year of staying in that magnificent mansion, there were still corridors that no one had stepped on. At the order of the lady of the mansion, each of the guests sat on a chair and waited for a reception. The servants and crew tried their best to get the best reception possible.

The food was brought and the maid placed the first dish in front of the lady of the mansion, followed by the other guests, and the last person to be received was the gentleman of the mansion, who was not usually taken seriously by the lady of the mansion. This bothered him greatly. At the lady's point, everyone started eating. While eating, the lady of the mansion was constantly giving advice and instructions to the man. To the extent that he felt very weak in front of others. Meanwhile, one of the maids, who had a beautiful face, came to the gentleman and said next to him and in the whispering ears, "Do you need anything?" The gentleman of the mansion, as if feeling secure in the face of all the frustration, responded kindly to the servant with a smile, and seemed very happy that there was someone in the crowd who realised his true worth and respected him. But the lady was so preoccupied with her orders that she never saw the scene. The party continued. It was about enlarging the mansion and the corridors from which noises and sounds echoed out for a long time.

The architect smiled and boldly announced, "We buried the workers who lost their lives during this period under hard work. Perhaps these are the ones who scream at night," he continued with a laugh. At that moment, the angry look of the lady of the mansion erased the laughter from the lips of the architect. After dinner, one by one, the guests left the hall, and the last one was the architect who thanked the hostess and promised to provide a way to increase the size of the mansion soon. Meanwhile, glances were exchanged between the servant and the gentleman of the mansion.

Suddenly, the lady of the house shouted, "You can get help from the gentleman to do this. He can at least be a good helper for you. After all, he must have something else to do besides going to the library and studying." In fact, the gentleman was accustomed to the humiliation of the lady of the mansion and did not say anything.

After the end of the party, the gentleman said good night to the lady of the house according to the routine every night and went to the library. Exactly where he spends most of his time every night and right next to the wall, from where the sound of screams could be heard by the lady of the mansion. That night, as usual, screams were heard. This time the lady dared and came to the wall with a candle in her hand. First, she went to the library to reduce her fear, because she knew that the gentleman was in the library. During this time, many people said that the lady of the house was suffering from some kind of illness and was talking to herself, which was a sign of some kind of illusion. It was even said among the servants that the lady was suffering from a kind of melancholy, and that it was better for her to be away from the mansion for a while, and that she should rest and leave the affairs of the mansion to the man. But no one had the strength or the courage to say that. For this reason, this conversation was silenced among all.

The lady of the mansion knocked on the door first. But she did not hear an answer. Slowly, the lady entered the library. No one was in the library. This was the first time the lady had come there, so she was more terrified. Entered slowly. She looked around and called her husband hesitantly. There was no one there. There was a little light coming out of a corner of the room. She went to it with fear and panic. She opened the door. This was exactly where she heard strange noises behind the wall every night. Now that she had come this far, she entered with hesitation. There was no one there, either. Inside the room was a chair and a simple bed. Suddenly, she heard the door closing behind her. She spun to escape, but the candle fell from her hands for a moment and went out. She immediately started shouting and asking for help. She did not know what had happened. In the meantime, she heard a familiar voice coming from behind the closed door. It was the gentleman's voice talking to her from behind the door.

"You have to rest for a long time. All this coercion and humiliation is enough. Throughout this time, wherever you progressed, I was by your side and always supported you. But I saw nothing but humiliation from you. You must see the result of your behaviour. Do not hurt yourself and do not shout. The room is well insulated and nothing but scary moans come out of it. The voices you heard during this time were fake voices to draw you here and bring you to your final home. I am the master of the mansion and I leave you here with your evil behaviour. Do not worry, the maid is aware of this and will bring you food every day. Although she is the first lady of the mansion from now."

The next morning, all the servants were in the main hall. The Master of Mansion stepped forward and began to speak, "From now on, I am the master of your mansion. The lady travelled for a long time due to illness and mental disorders and for treatment. On the other hand, the maid is considered as the new lady of this mansion till whenever my wife can regain her health and return."

Endless Waiting

Endless Waiting

A tall man in a white robe and green hat was riding towards the city with his army on a white horse. People were counting the moments to see him. The poor spread out their mats and the rich set up special chairs in front of the city gates to bow down when they saw him. Some were happy and some were sad because no one knew what awaited them. City watchers noticed a courier coming. He informed everyone that a courier was coming. They opened the gate. The courier entered the town and said, "He will be here a little late. Wait for him." Politicians were happy with the news, but they knew he was on his way again and could be a threat to them.

Excitement and fear were everywhere; people were waiting for him more than ever. The politicians had arranged a meeting to make sure that there was no revolution with his arrival. They considered all aspects of the work. They set up a meeting table with expensive gifts to entice him and pull him towards them to be safe. Hours passed. The promised time has come. As he had promised, he stood behind the city gates with a large army and ordered his troops to set up tents outside the city. He had trained and fought men, and whoever stood up to them would end in death.

It took some time for them to stay outside the gates. No one knew what he was up to. The gates were open to him. He entered the city with a small bodyguard. Everyone bowed to him and the elders of the city kissed his hand and gave him beautiful gifts. But because of his simplicity, he did not accept either. There were only a few guards around him, and they guarded him vigorously. But he walked boldly and without paying attention to them. He moved towards the palace. The palace made of gold was so beautiful that everyone who saw it was fascinated. But he could easily see the aura of sin that pervaded the palace.

He went to the meeting table, pulled back the chair, and sat down. The table was full of gifts, drinks, and food. Politicians sat there talking to him, offering him power and cooperation. He listened to them carefully. But in the end, he did not accept any of them and said angrily, "I am tired. I will rest today and I will make my decision tomorrow." He returned to the camp. There was a warm tent with a suitable mattress. He went to it and lay on it. It was his work that made him famous for his simplicity. He lived a simple life to maintain his reputation for the rest of his life.

A group of people prepared a lecture table for him. Soldiers stood on all rooftops and around the rostrum for his safety. He appeared on the podium. He began to speak. It was a strange speech. Everyone was terrified because he had promised to massacre those who had sinned. Some people committed suicide out of fear. He managed to kill half of the sinners without straining anyone's blood. He smiled bitterly and ordered the city to be set on fire and the sinners to be burned. People hid in their houses in fear and buried the bodies of their loved ones. They were frightened and ate them because they did not have enough graves and food. People who wanted to escape and leave were quickly beheaded. No one dared to leave the city; one of the best cities in the world, it was now a ruined land. Some revolted and tried to overthrow him, but were quickly suppressed.

Suddenly, he opened his eyes, realised that he was just asleep, and wiped away his cold sweat. He took some water from the table. He put on his battle uniform and went to his army and suddenly ordered an attack. It was as if what he was dreaming was coming true. He ordered them to take only the palace. The palace was captured. He sat on the throne and thought about his dream. He then ruthlessly ordered that the poor could plunder the rich and equate themselves with them. A kind of justice that was unique to him. But he did not know that this would disrupt the order of the city and create chaos. Someone who had been prudent all these years had now killed several thousand people. He slapped his hand on his face and stared into the corner, upset at why he had done so.

But his violence did not end there. A few days later, he ordered all the guilty people to be killed in the town square. There was blood in the city. His dream was coming true. The city was on fire. There was no cemetery for corpses, and people ate each other like cannibals for food. He just wanted sinners gone so that justice could be done on earth. He thought to himself that he might be guilty himself. He came to his senses and thought that no sin had been committed. He was the twelfth to come after years as promised by his predecessors, and all the people were waiting for him to bring justice. But they did not have a correct understanding of his justice. He wanted justice, but for some time, he had disrupted the order of the city. The city smelled of death. Thousands of corpses were lying on the ground and people were eating them. After months, the disease came and caused many deaths. He did not know what to do when he came to make peace, disturbing the peace and tranquillity. He had lost hope.

He pretended to be simple, but he was greedy from within. A selfish person whom no one loved. His soldiers were sharpening their swords to capture another city and free themselves from the pressure of starvation by looting. He invaded and plundered another city, turning it into a ruin. He was a tyrant. He beheaded hundreds of people alone every day. Because he thought they were sinners. He had created a ritual for himself that everyone had to follow. Anyone who did not follow that ritual would be beheaded. He had killed several thousand people.

He had found enemies. His enemies were from other lands that were now united. So they sent people to talk to the woman he had just married. They secretly went to the woman with a large amount of gold and met her. The woman was given many promises to kill her husband. The glamour of gold had forced her to kill her husband. However, in fact, she did not agree with her husband. She took the poison from them and poured it for him. Her husband drank a sip of it and an hour later he died. People were happy with his death.

A few years later, the people forgot about these events and waited for the next commander.

Futile Attemp

Futile Attempt

One day, a man known for his chivalry decided to rise up. He wanted to avenge the blood of his ancestors. He suffered greatly from the religion that was imposed on him. He had invited many people to the uprising. He travelled to other lands and invited the people there to this uprising. It was hard work, but it was possible. He had come with thousands of people to attack lands near and far. After weeks of hard military training, they were ready to attack. He had brave commanders. He invited them to the meeting. There were war plans on the table. All eyes were on the hands of the gentleman. "Our main goal is to invade and capture them because they are the ones who questioned our identities many years ago. The time has come for revenge. We must get rid of superstition," he said, referring to the borders of their immediate homeland. "They have made us weak, superstitious people. Let us unite and achieve a land free of the religious superstitions imposed on us."

The gentleman made a plan with the help of his commanders. With this plan, they would definitely win.

Happiness and good spirits were seen in all the soldiers. Especially this time, people also supported them and tried to forget the wrong beliefs. They went to the enemy's land. The enemy was standing in front of them. They were both armed to the teeth. There was no fear in the enemy army. It was a desert place and there was no water there, so they should have captured the enemy country sooner. A strange silence filled the place. The two divisions clashed when suddenly the gentleman ordered the attack. The archers threw their arrows and then took their swords and spears and attacked the enemy army. It was a bloody war. Blood was everywhere. All the wells that had dried up were now full of blood.

The gentleman won the first battle. The gentleman looked at the corpses around him and laughed bitterly. The commanders brought the captives. The gentleman ordered them to be set on fire in order to carry out the revenge he had promised. The captives burned in the fire as they struggled to save themselves. The enemy army was hit hard. They had reached behind the city gates. The city gate was the enemy's last defensive barrier and it was difficult to penetrate. At times, the gentleman became anxious and wanted to end the war, but when he remembered his ancestors, he became very angry.

The day of war had come. The gentleman moved his army towards the gate of the palace. Enemy armies fired arrows and bows that had been stained with fire at the gentleman's army. The gentleman's army had been hit hard by the arrows. The defensive wall of the city was very strong and they could hardly cross it. The enemy had built defensive tools that prevented them from entering. This time, the gentleman's army suffered a severe stroke. So the gentleman ordered a retreat to regroup. A meeting was held to find the way to the gate. No one had any idea when suddenly, a man from the enemy army came to the gentleman without a weapon. The soldier wanted to point out the weaknesses of the defensive wall. Everyone was eagerly staring at the soldier's mouth.

The soldier said, "I have come here for a deal. If I give you information, will I get anything in return?"

"What do you want?" said the gentleman suddenly.

"I want to have a position in my land," said the soldier. The gentleman accepted.

"There is an underground canal through which you can enter the land. But that canal is behind a mountain several kilometres away. I will take you there," the soldier said.

The gentleman went to the underground canal with a thousand people. They got there. The soldier continued, "You enter the canal. There are few guards there. Do not worry. You will cross a crossroads. When you cross, go to the right. There are traps set there that no one can cross. But if someone goes and can pull down the drain chain, the water is drained and you can go through it. I put a few people in there to open the entrance for you. Don't worry about anything."

The gentleman entered the canal with his army. He also took the soldier with him to take his life in case of betrayal. As the soldier said, he saw people guarding the canal. He sent some to kill them without anyone realising it. The soldiers killed them and reached a crossroads. According to the soldier, they went to the right. They came to a pit where the water was all over. He sent some people to break the chains. Several people drowned on the way, but one person was able to get there and pull the chain. The water went to another canal and the gentleman passed through it with the army and reached the gate that the soldier had opened. He smiled bitterly and ordered the attack. A thousand soldiers went to the gate to open the gate for the army. The gate opened. The gentleman's army entered there and began to fight.

Not so long after, the gentleman won. He went to the well of holy water and dumped all the corpses there. The well smelled bad. It could not be used for several years. He went to the holy house and broke a piece of stone and mocked the religion of his enemies. He took the stone to his country. He killed the people who had the religion of his enemies and sent their money to his land so that the people could live in peace. Several years passed and a large number of enemies were hiding somewhere. He had been waiting for a torment that had never befallen him for several years. Because he had broken the sacred stone and taken it to another land. He was very happy. Suddenly, it was reported that they had a revolt in their own land and wanted to change the ruler. Suddenly, he slapped his hand on the table and said, "I did everything for their comfort. What is the reason for this? I mean, was all this effort to avenge your ancestors futile?"

"They want to fire you for mocking the religion. They like what they're used to before," Pike said. The people of the enemy land, who saw the situation well, revolted. The land of the gentleman joined the rebellions of the enemy of the gentleman and destroyed the army and the gentleman.

A few years later, they were the most miserable people in the world and followers of other religions.

Castle of Panic

Castle of Panic

Four tourists decided to go to the city cafe to discuss future trips. They had known each other for several years. They approached the cafe. They looked at the cafe. The waiters in suits were ready to take the order. The facade of the cafe was made of pinewood. They were offered to come here. They entered the cafe. There was a number on the table. The chairs were made of cedar wood with special patterns and drawings on them. They took a good look around them. Two people were near them, and there were several empty tables waiting for customers. There were two floors. It was in the corner of the kitchen. The waiter came and handed them the cafe menu and said, "Please choose, I'll be back." Another waiter came and cleaned the table. He wiped the table several times.

The first waiter came and said, "Well, what do you want?"

"Two cups of coffee and two cups of tea," said one. The waiter registered them and read their order again. They confirmed. The waiter went to the kitchen.

They started talking. "What a beautiful view," said one of them.

"Well, we listened to one of the townspeople."

Another said, "It has a beautiful view, but it should be seen that their coffee and tea are also delicious." Others confirmed his words. The waiter put their coffee and tea on the table with a strange, beautiful tray. He lit a candle with the lighter he had with him. They were talking about their strange journeys.

"You remember we went to a scary forest? It was a wonderful place."

Another said, "No, I do not agree. The beach was scarier. We almost finished all the scary places in the world and nothing happened to us. We put an end to the superstitions of scary places and gave a strong reason; that was that we always came back safe. There was a swamp in the forest where everything was sinking, but they thought their ghosts had stolen them." They began to drink with a laugh. They slowly tasted and enjoyed the drink. There were beautiful designs on it that surprised everyone.

They were about to leave the cafe when suddenly two people close to them said, "Excuse me, gentlemen, we wanted to say something interesting that will surprise you."

"I'm sorry we don't have much time," said one.

He said, "I know, but you like this discussion. I inadvertently heard what you had to say and realised that you are a tourist. It was clear from your words that you are also a brave man. It's called the Castle of Panic. Everyone goes there, never comes back or goes crazy if they come back. I wanted to see if you can go there and find the secret of the Castle of Panic, which has not been discovered for hundreds of years. Just a warning! Take a lot with you, because you may get caught and need food."

They said, "Did you go there yourself, that now you warn us? You say that everyone is gone, never came back or is dead. Dead and mad people cannot tell the truth."

"Yes, we went, but we have only been able to go near the castle of Panic. If we had dared, we would have discovered the secret," he said. The tourists had chosen one for difficult decisions so that he would always think and decide. In fact, he was entrusted with the smartest member of the team who drew all the travel plans. He stared at the coffee cups still on the table. He must have thought well. One wrong decision could jeopardise the whole group. But he was not wrong. He focused carefully. Suddenly, the waiter came in front of the cup and took the cups. He also took the money on the table for coffee.

His line of thought was torn. He had made his decision and wanted to reveal the secret of the Castle of Panic and gain another honour for himself. "Write the address of the place for me on paper," he said. The two went to the counter and got paper and a pen. "It is great. We haven't had any scary or mysterious experiences in a long time. Obviously, there are other mysterious places."

"I'm glad you accepted," said one member of the group. He took the paper with the address written on it.

"Why don't you come with us? If you come with us, things will be easier. Because we will be six with you," said the group leader.

"No, thank you. We are not going there anymore. It is not our business. But I suggest you rent a car," he said.

The group thanked them and they left the cafe. They went to the taxi. They gave the address of the store that had everything. They entered the store. They were seriously looking for tools. They bought a lot of food. They went to the counter and suddenly one of them said, "We have to listen to the two of them. Remember, we have to get candles, flashlights, matches, and tools to be comfortable." The boss confirmed his words. They went back to the carefully arranged shelves with the names of the products written on them to make it easier for customers to buy and not to have trouble buying. Due to the good quality of the goods, there was a low price, which made them buy all kinds of goods.

Suddenly, one of the members said, "Look there. There is a discount section. Pay attention to the 30% discount!" Suddenly, everyone went to the discount section. They bought it for two months. Everything was great. They did not lose much money. Nowhere had they seen goods so cheap. Everyone praised their purchase and laughed at how much they made. They could even buy from this store when they travel to other places. They went to the counter of the shop. They put a lot of things on the table. The counter manager called the boss. The boss came and looked at the purchased goods. He could not believe what he saw. He greeted them quickly and treated them well.

The cashier gave them a discount card at the order of the store manager, saying, "You can buy from this store at any time with a discount written in it, and with full satisfaction from here. Come here again. You are our best customers. We are happy, please, come again."

The group leader thanked him and told one of the group members, "Let's go and rent a car. The car must be able to withstand the desert. Check the car wheels. Check all the car tools. There should be nothing less. Gasoline and everything. Check, we're waiting here in the store. The shop next door is renting a car. Just don't sabotage without me." The band members went to the car dealership. The group leader paid the bills. He went out of the shop with a smile and waited. Their hands were full of goods. Their hands could no longer hold all those things. So they laid it on the ground and waited. Suddenly, a large car suitable for the desert came. Yes, he was a member of the group. A white car with smoky glass that looked perfect. There was a part for the car to put the food in so that it would not be damaged. Everything was complete. They were ready to travel. They had to go there quickly because they were very curious. They could not stand it anymore. They quickly got into the car. Smiling, they took their drinks and drank them to change the taste in their mouths. They came up with a plan. They predicted the routes from the map and set off. They were stuck in traffic because they were in the city centre. From the very beginning, traffic was everywhere. The traffic was unbearable. After a while, they entered the side road and drove for several hours. It was afternoon. They were near the castle. They had fallen asleep. Everyone was asleep, even the driver. The driver pushed the car aside, gasoline was running out. Of course, he had thought about everything. He had brought gasoline with him. He opened the trunk and poured gasoline into the tank of his car. After a few minutes, he looked around. A desert route was inhabited by scorpions and snakes. There were a lot of cacti there. He looked at the ground and saw that a snake was approaching. It was dry. He had to run away quickly. He was out of breath. He quickly went to the car and got inside. He closed the door and took a deep breath.

He repeated under his breath, "I was lucky. I might have lost my life." He turned on the car, still not breathing. He was asleep. He picked up his drink and drank. He was driving at a slow speed. It was several kilometres away, only a few kilometres could not be speeded due to the dirt road and the possibility of a puncture. As the car wheels moved, dust rose and filled the ground. The car was no longer white. There was a lot of dust on the car, which changed the colour of the car. He cleaned the windshield to see better. They were approaching. There was no way. He woke the group. Everyone picked up some food and ate. The car started moving again, it was almost night. It was dark. The only light that marked the road was the car light and the moonlight. The castle wall was in front of them. Suddenly, one of the car wheels went down. It was in the hole. They do not have any choice. They were facing the castle. They got out of the car.

They said, "We will take the car back." They turned on the flashlight and headed for gasoline and wood. They lit the fire. It was lit everywhere. There was no need for a flashlight anymore. They turned off the car so that the gas would not run out. They took the best tents out of the box and set up tents. They also brought a sleeping bag. They even took their wallets to the tent.

"I want to go to the bathroom," said one.

Another said, "I want to go around, to see what's going on." Two others sat in the tent. The two were having tea in the tent. Suddenly, something like a ghost entered the tent, tea fell from their hands and spilt on their feet. They were scared. They shouted. They wanted help, their hands were shaking. Suddenly, they saw that their friend was laughing. White sheets fell off him. They saw that he was a member of the group. They started laughing.

"Are you scared?" he said. And they laughed again. They forgot the pain in their legs and poured tea again. Suddenly, someone else came in. It was like a soul; like their friend's previous joke. They laughed again.

The boss said, "Stop it. I know who you are. You make so many strange jokes. I know you went to the bathroom too." And they laughed again and drank their tea. "Won't you take off your clothes?" said the boss.

Suddenly, a voice came. It was the sound of the pants being zipped. Their friend entered the tent. He was a member. So who was it who stood before them like a ghost? They were scared. They panicked. The ghost was still making a strange sound. Suddenly, another ghost-like him attacked them. They all fled quickly and left all their belongings behind. They fell down. They did not even have a chance to put on their shoes.

Suddenly, the sheets fell from the faces of the two ghosts. They were the two people who offered them this trip in the cafe. They said to themselves, "Everyone in the cafe said they were brave. But they were nothing. They listened to us very carefully. We made six months with this car and all the equipment and money. It was a really good plan." Laughing, they put their belongings in the car and left.

Years Later

(Answer to the story Beyond the Wheat Field, from the book Wounded Thoughts by International Author, Majid Karimi)

He was driving and looking at the deserts around him. As far as he could see, he had nothing but a desert in front of him. He thought about it and was happy that he had been able to buy the half-alive cottage of his famous and beloved author. Perhaps its heir was reluctant to keep this dilapidated heritage or even no one was willing to buy a hut in this desert.

He was willing to pay any amount to find himself in that hut. A magical hut that was considered a castle and its heir saw nothing but ruins in it. He had been accustomed to his writings since he was a child, and soon flames of fire ignited in him so that he could become a writer, too. However, the fate of the author was bitter for him.

The scorching sun was getting hotter by the minute, deepening his thinking. Cold sweat was sitting on his forehead. There was no other way. He knew that he would soon achieve his long-cherished dream. Although he did not know how to work with tools and did not lift anything heavier than a pen, he provided the means by which he might be able to revive the hut with his limited power.

Finally, he reached the hut. There was nothing left but broken rubble with a dry wheat field in front of him. He stood for a while. He stared around. There were tears in his eyes. He did not believe that he was watching such a scene in front of his eyes. Now he understood why he was called crazy. He felt that he liked to look at that dry wheat field infinitely, even if there were no more golden clusters of wheat. At the same time, the wind began to blow and the soil covered the whole landscape. He decided to go to the broken stairs of the hut. He took the key out of his pocket and put it in a rusty lock. His efforts were in vain, as the door opened with the slightest push. He took a deep breath and entered. He looked around. All of the author's belongings were still left in place, and he could see the dust well on the author's simple desk. While he was overwhelmed with excitement, he felt sad in his heart. Thinking that he could repair the hut in a limited time, he carried his belongings from the car into the hut. He put his books on the desk. First, put the author's books; books that were supposedly written on the same desk. He looked at the name of his author. Now he was in exactly the same hut where the books of his beloved author had been written. After a while, he placed his books next to the same books and was excited to see that the name of his books shone next to the names of the books of his favourite author.

Suddenly, his eyes fell on an envelope. Apparently, no one had seen it before. He went to it involuntarily. He picked it up. Didn't know if he should open it or not? Maybe it would have been better to pass it on to the heir of the hut. But curiosity did not allow him. He picked it up and opened it with trembling hands, which he thought was a manuscript of the author. His eyes ran on the paper. He did not have a correct understanding of what he was reading. He read it several times:

I would like to go,
To go to the desert,
To go with a tired heart,
To a desert full of loneliness,
To go to the thirsty, impatient heart,
And where no one is…

He sat there. He put his hand on his face and wiped the moisture from under his eyes. He looked out the window.

He was worried. He went to the window. He pulled back the dusty curtain and looked out over the desert, which was once a golden wheat field. He saw black spots that he did not know where they were going. They were moving in every direction. They had to choose their path; towards the truth or towards ignorance.

He was no longer interested in looking out the window. He no longer liked to look at the black spots that preferred ignorance to truth and were immersed in the red soil of the desert. So he pulled back the curtain as quickly as possible and went to the writer's bed, where he lay down on the hard wooden bed with a bitter smile. Now he was lying where his beloved author had been lying. He mocked the heir of the hut, who valued the author's work other than his income. Now subconsciously the poem of the letter was pounding in his mind and for this reason, he could not sleep. He thought he could publish it. He took a deep breath and calmed himself with this thought and fell into a deep sleep. He could hear the wind blowing through the timber joints of the hut, and they were restless; it was as if they wanted to inform him of something. He opened his eyes. He looked around. He heard a voice calling him to the table. Unwillingly, he got up and subconsciously picked up the pen and began writing without any awareness. He spent hours writing; without knowing what he was writing.

The days were repeated and the nights came and the papers were stored on the wooden desk and floor of the hut without any scratches. He did not even know what he wrote. He also believed in having a shadow in his life that moved in front of a lantern. He was not alone anymore. He talked to the shadow in front of him for hours and wrote under the lantern at night. The shadow never left him. He also no longer wanted to look out the window or repair the hut.

A long time has passed; maybe years, unfinished meetings, and the blackened papers that surrounded him. Little by little, he saw the presence of the shadow fade away. He felt that perhaps his mission was coming to an end. Then he got up and pulled back the curtain. There was no more shadow. Yes, he was ready to go beyond the wheat field. He was happy. Unconsciously, his feet moved him across the wheat field. He passed through the golden clusters of the wheat in his imagination. In the distance, he saw the author waving to him and waiting for him. He also did not return from the other side of the wheat field.

The present book, called The Grey Mind (a collection of short stories), is taken from the daily conditions of every human being that he sometimes encounters during his life and is considered as a great challenge for him. But why humans find themselves in such a critical situation is a reflection of the behavioural complexities that lead them to a world far removed from individual imagination and to a world that is more like a hell that endangers their peace of mind.